Flowers for Mami Unicorn!

adapted by Christine Ricci
based on the screenplay "Isa's Unicorn Flowers"
written by Rosemary Contreras
illustrated by Victoria Miller

Simon Spotlight/Nickelodeon
New York   London   Toronto   Sydney

Based on the TV series *Dora the Explorer*® as seen on Nick Jr.®

SIMON SPOTLIGHT
An imprint of Simon & Schuster Children's Publishing Division
1230 Avenue of the Americas, New York, New York 10020
© 2010 Viacom International Inc. All rights reserved. NICK JR., *Dora the Explorer*, and all related titles,
logos, and characters are registered trademarks of Viacom International Inc.
For information about special discounts for bulk purchases, please contact
Simon & Schuster Special Sales at 1-866-506-1949 or business@simonandschuster.com.
Manufactured in the United States of America, 0209 LAK
First Edition 2 4 6 8 10 9 7 5 3 1
ISBN 978-1-4169-9064-2

¡Hola! I'm Dora! Isa and I are planting special flowers. Do you want to plant flowers with us? Great! Isa has special Umbrella Flower seeds, Butterfly Flower seeds, Beanstalk Flower seeds, and Unicorn Flower seeds. To make the flowers grow, let's say *"¡Crezcan, flores!"*

The garden is filled with flowers. They're so pretty! *¡Qué bonita!*

Look! A rainbow came out. There's something at the end of the rainbow. What is it?

It's a unicorn! His name is Unicornio, and he wants to bring some Unicorn Flowers home to his *mami*. Unicorn Flowers look just like Unicornio's horn. Do you see them?

Unicornio has to ride the rainbow home so he can give the flowers to his *mami*. But the rainbow is going away. We have to help Unicornio get to the rainbow. Who do we ask for help when we don't know which way to go? Map!

Map says that we'll need to go past the Dragon's Cave and over the Troll Bridge to get to the rainbow. Let's go!

We're on our way to the Dragon's Cave. Look! It's Boots and Tico, playing soccer. But here comes a big rain cloud. They can't play soccer in the rain!

I know! Isa's bag has lots of special seeds. Which special flower can block out the rain?

¡Sí! Umbrella Flowers can block the rain. Good thinking!
Let's sprinkle the seeds on the soccer field. Now, to make the
Umbrella Flowers grow, say *"¡Crezcan, flores!"*

¡Fantástico! The Umbrella Flowers blocked the rain so Boots and Tico can keep playing soccer. Now we need to find the Dragon's Cave! Do you see it?

Uh-oh! The dragon is blocking the path. We've got to get past the dragon so Unicornio can get home to his *mami*. My friend Mei has read lots of dragon stories. Maybe she can help us get past the dragon. Do you see Mei?

Mei says that dragons love a special dragon dance. If we do the dance, the dragon will get out of our way!

Let's do the dragon dance! First stomp your feet, then flap your arms, and then roar! Look! The dragon is letting us pass!

Oh, no! On the way to the Troll Bridge, Swiper swiped the Unicorn Flowers and threw them into the bushes. We've got to find the flowers so Unicornio can give them to his *mami*. Do you see the flowers?

You found the flowers! *¡Gracias!*
Come on! Let's take Unicornio to the end of the rainbow so he can get home to his *mami*!

We made it to the Troll Bridge! But the Grumpy Old Troll won't let us cross unless we solve his riddle! Will you help us solve the riddle? Great! He's asking us: "What grows from seeds when the rain showers?"

Flowers! You solved the riddle! The Grumpy Old Troll really likes purple flowers. Do you see any purple flower seeds in Isa's bag? Great! Now say *"crezcan flores"* to make them grow!

The Grumpy Old Troll loves the purple flowers!
We've got to get Unicornio to the rainbow. Do you see a rainbow? There it is—way up there! How are we going to get up that high?

Isa has some Beanstalk Flower seeds in her bag. Do you see the Beanstalk Flower seeds? Great! What do we say to get the flowers to grow? Yeah! *¡Crezcan, flores!*

It worked! We just have to climb up the Beanstalk Flowers to reach the rainbow! But some leaves are too small for Unicornio to climb! He needs our help to find leaves big enough for him to climb on. Let's find all the big leaves and show Unicornio the way to the top of the beanstalk.

Oh, no! Isa fell through the rainbow! We have to rescue her and catch the Unicorn Flowers!

We rescued Isa, crossed the rainbow, and made it to Unicorn Forest. Do you see *Mami* Unicorn?

Unicornio is so happy to see his *mami*. He made her a Unicorn
Flower necklace. How sweet!

We helped Unicornio bring Unicorn Flowers to his *mami*! What a magical day! We did it!